KLIPPITY KLOP

LITTLE, BROWN AND COMPANY
BOSTON, TORONTO

KLIPPITY KLOP

BY ED EMBERLEY

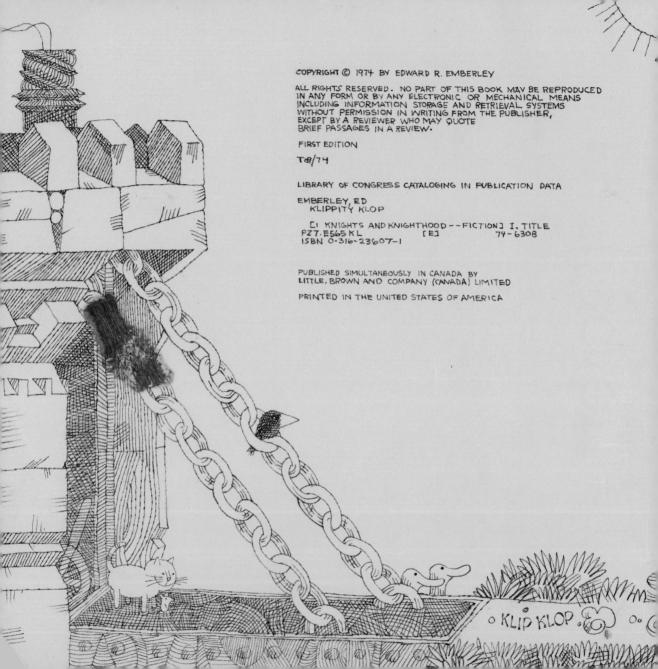

FIRST EDITION

T 9/74

LIBRARY OF CONGRESS CATALOGING IN PUBLICATION DATA

EMBERLEY, ED
  KLIPPITY KLOP

  [1 KNIGHTS AND KNIGHTHOOD--FICTION] I. TITLE
PZ7.E565 KL   [E]   74-6308
ISBN 0-316-23607-1

PUBLISHED SIMULTANEOUSLY IN CANADA BY
LITTLE, BROWN AND COMPANY (CANADA) LIMITED

PRINTED IN THE UNITED STATES OF AMERICA

KLIP KLOP.

PRINCE KRISPIN
AND DUMPLING
WENT FOR A RIDE.

KLIPPITY. KLOP   KLIP.KLOP   KLIPPITY.KLOP

THEY CAME TO A BRIDGE
AND RODE OVER IT,

THEY CAME TO A STREAM
AND RODE ACROSS IT,

KLOP KLIPPITY KLOP.

KERPLASH KERPLOSH KERPLASH KERPLOSH KERPLISH

KERPLOSH KERPLOOSH KERP

KLIP. KLOP. KLIPPITY

THEY CAME TO A FIELD
AND RODE THROUGH IT,

KLOP " KWASH " KWASH " KWISH " KWISH " KWASH " KWISH " KWASH " KWISH " KWASH " KWISH

THEY CAME TO A GRAVELY HILL
AND RODE DOWN IT,

THEY CAME TO A ROCKY HILL
AND RODE UP IT,

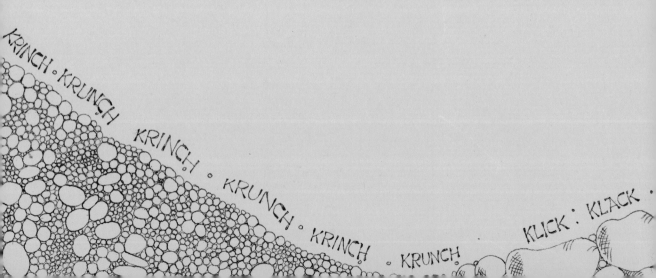

KRINCH · KRUNCH

KRINCH · KRUNCH · KRINCH · KRUNCH

KLICK · KLACK

THEY CAME TO A CAVE
AND LOOKED IN ...

A DRAGON
LOOKED OUT...

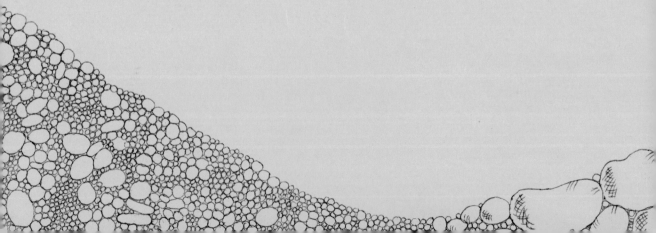

WELL!! THE DRAGON
DID NOT HAVE TO YELL TWICE.
DUMPLING TURNED AND RAN:

DOWN THE ROCKY HILL,
   UP THE GRAVELY HILL,

KRINCHITY.
KRUNCHITY. KRUNCHITY. KLACKITY

KLICKITY KLACKITY KLICKITY

KWISH KWISH KWISH KWISH KWISH KWIS

THROUGH THE FIELD,

KWISH. KWISH KWISH KWISH KWISH KWISH KWISH KWISH KWISH KWISH
KWISH

ACROSS THE STREAM,

KERPLASH KERPLASH KERPLASH
KERPLASH KERPLASH KERPLASH
KERPLASH KERPLASH

KLIPPITY KLIPPITY KLIPPITY KLIPPITY KLIPPITY KLIPPITY KLIPPITY

OVER THE BRIDGE,

INTO THE CASTLE...
AND
CLOSED THE DOOR!